A STORYTELLER'S STORY

by

Rafe Martin

photographs by

Jill Krementz

Richard C. Owen Publishers, Inc.
Katonah, New York

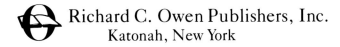

Thanks to Cobblestone School, Rochester, New York.

Text copyright © 1992 by Rafe Martin
Photographs copyright © 1992 by Jill Krementz

Richard C. Owen Publishers, Inc.
135 Katonah Avenue
Katonah, New York 10536

Library of Congress Cataloging-in-Publication Data

Martin, Rafe, 1946—
    A storyteller's story / by Rafe Martin ; photographs by Jill
Krementz.
        p.   cm. —(Meet the author)
    Summary: Children's author Rafe Martin describes his life and
writing process and how they are interwoven.
    ISBN 0-913461-03-2
    1. Martin, Rafe, 1946-   —Biography—Juvenile literature.
    2. Authors, American—20th century—Biography—Juvenile literature.
    3. Children's stories—Authorship—Juvenile literature.
    [1. Martin, Rafe, 1946–   . 2. Authors, American.] I. Krementz,
Jill, ill. II. Title. III. Series: Meet the author (Katonah, N.Y.)
PS3563.A7276Z475   1992
813'.54—dc20
[B]   92-7794

The text type was set in Caslon 540.
Production supervision by Janice Boland
Book design by Kenneth J. Hawkey

Printed in the United States of America

9 8 7 6 5 4 3 2

To tomorrow's authors
and storytellers

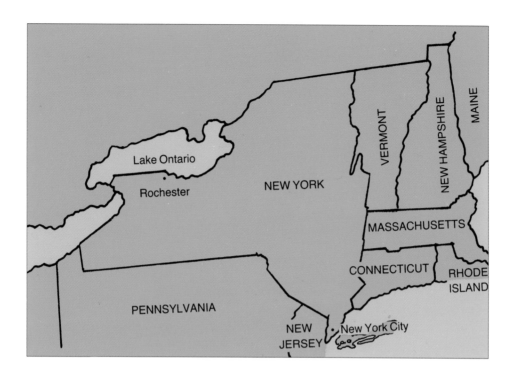

Dear Friends,
I'm an author and a storyteller.
Like you, I became a storyteller
as soon as I could talk,
and an author when I first wrote stories
in school.
My home is in Rochester, New York,
a city on the shores of Lake Ontario,
one of the Great Lakes
between the United States and Canada.

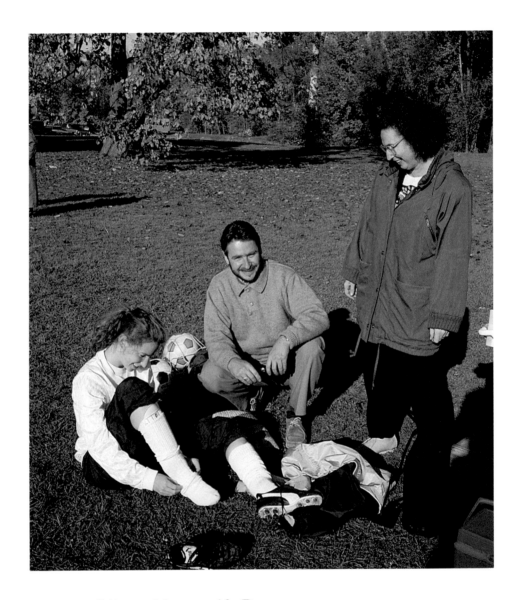

I live with my wife Rose,
who teaches first and second graders,
our daughter Ariya, who loves to play soccer,

our Siberian Husky, Snowball,
and two cats, Mocha and Girlsie.
Our son Jacob has graduated from college
and no longer lives at home.
He's thinking of being a writer, too.

In the morning Rose and Ariya go off to school
and my writing day begins.
When I work on a new idea
I first picture the story in my mind,
then I write it.
Then I rewrite, carefully choosing words
that will help my readers
and my illustrator see the characters
and the story for themselves.
I rewrite a story many times,
to get it just right.

Sometimes a story almost seems to write itself.
Then my fingers can hardly keep up
with the flow of words in my mind.
It's very exciting to feel this happen.
Some mornings I spend my time
editing the stories I've already begun.
I walk around the room reading them out loud,
listening to the way they sound.

In the middle of the day
I stop for lunch.
Because I'm a vegetarian,
I eat foods like enchiladas, spinach pie,
tofu, spaghetti, soups, salads, and cheese.

After lunch, I go back to writing.
I also answer phone calls, go through my mail,
and I read.

I do research for my stories
in my home library, in public libraries,
in bookstores, and in nearby museums.

When I write about an animal,
(my favorite ones are gorillas,
whales, and woolly mammoths)
I often draw and paint it.
Imagining what it's like to be that animal
helps me tell and write the story.
But I don't illustrate my books.
I choose illustrators
whose styles match the pictures
I see in my imagination.
Stephen Gammel, Ed Young, and David Shannon
are three of my favorite illustrators.

After I've been working
in my office for a long time,
I like to go outside
for fresh air and exercise.
I take short bicycle rides near my home,
or I drive to a nearby lake
and paddle my kayak.

Ideas for stories come to me
while I watch the birds fly,
the clouds drift, and the water
swirl around my paddle.
Sometimes ideas come to me
when I'm sitting quietly at home
in the evening listening to music.
Sometimes they come from stories
my mother told me when I was young,
and from stories my relatives told
at family gatherings.

One of my stories came from a memory
of a favorite place.
When I was eight years old,
I lived in New York City.
There was a big boulder
my friends and I called Elephant Rock.
When we climbed up on it,
it seemed to come alive.
I felt like I was riding on a real elephant.

Years later I went back to my old neighborhood.
I wanted to show Jacob and Ariya Elephant Rock,
but it was gone.
My boulder had been bulldozed away!
I wrote *Will's Mammoth* so everyone who reads it
can share my ride on Elephant Rock.
But in my story I changed Elephant Rock
to a woolly mammoth.
I always wished I could see a woolly mammoth,
and in stories, wishes can come true.

Because I'm also a storyteller,
there are days when I travel.
Some days I go to nearby schools
to tell my stories.

Some days I fly to schools that are far away.
I've told my stories all across the United States,
from Connecticut to California.
Sometimes I even fly as far away
as Hawaii and Japan.
It's a good thing I like airplanes!

Some of the stories I tell
are called traditional tales.
These are stories that have been told
for a long time by other people.
Foolish Rabbit's Big Mistake
is my way of telling a tale from India
that's almost three thousand years old.

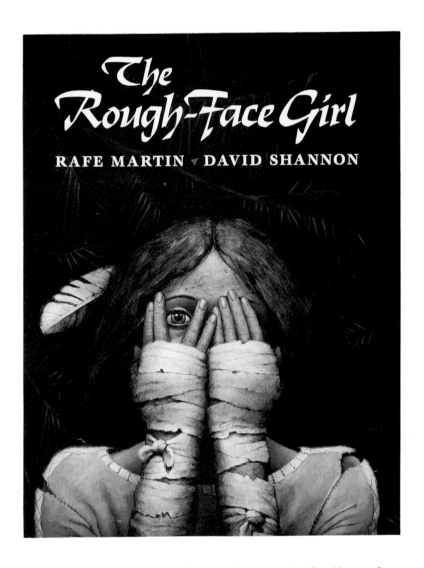

The Rough-Face Girl is an Algonquin Indian tale
that's very much like Cinderella.
I told both these stories many times
before I wrote them as books.

I also tell original tales.
These are stories that have never been told
by anyone else but me.
Will's Mammoth is an original tale.
I have others
that I haven't published as books yet,
but I'm working on them.

After I tell my stories
children ask me questions.
One question they often ask is
"How long does it take you to write a book?"

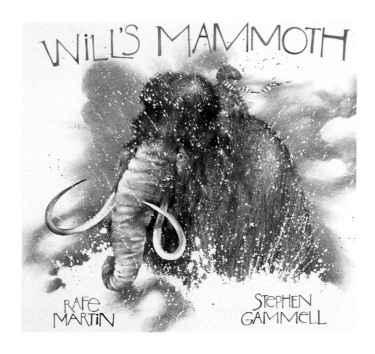

Some books take months
and some take years to write.
Will's Mammoth took either
three years or thirty seconds to write!
It began as a long story.
I worked on it for three years
but it just didn't seem right.
Then, suddenly, in about thirty seconds
I saw how the book could work.
It didn't need lots of words.
It could be told in pictures!

Another question that I'm often asked is
"Did you write a lot when you were young?"
Not really, but I read a lot,
and I still do.

I read in the evening after supper,
and before we fall asleep
Rose and I often read aloud to each other.

One of the most important questions
that I'm asked is
"Do you like what you do?"
My answer is
I love being an author and a storyteller.
Here's how you
can become one, too.

Picture a story in your mind.
Tell it to your parents,
your brothers, your sisters,
your classmates, your friends.
Draw illustrations for your story.
Write words for your illustrations.
Have fun making your book and
enjoy sharing your story.
Good luck and best wishes!
Your friend,

Rafe Martin

Rafe Martin

Other Books by Rafe Martin

The Boy of the Seals (1993); *Dear as Salt* (1993); *Foolish Rabbit's Big Mistake*; *The Hungry Tigress*; *The Rough-Face Girl*; *Will's Mammoth*; and his audiotapes *The Boy Who Loved Mammoths and Other Tales*; *Ghostly Tales of Japan*.

About the Photographer

Jill Krementz is an award-winning photojournalist. She has written and photographed over two dozen books. Rafe Martin took this picture of Jill.

Acknowledgments

Illustrations on pages 17 and 25 by Stephen Gammell reprinted by permission of G.P. Putnam's Sons from *Will's Mammoth* by Rafe Martin, illustrations copyright © 1989 by Stephen Gammell. Illustration on page 21 by David Shannon reprinted by permission of G.P. Putnam's Sons from *The Rough-Face Girl* by Rafe Martin, illustrations copyright © 1992 by David Shannon. Photographs on pages 1 and 16 appear courtesy of Rochester Museum and Science Center, Rochester, New York.

Meet the Author titles

Rafe Martin   *A Storyteller's Story*
Cynthia Rylant   *Best Wishes*
Jane Yolen   *A Letter from Phoenix Farm*